T

BOOK OF

CATS

A Red Fox Book

Published by Random House Children's Books
20 Vauxhall Bridge Road, London SW1V 2SA

A division of The Random House Group Ltd
London Melbourne Sydney Auckland
Johannesburg and agencies throughout the world

1 3 5 7 9 10 8 6 4 2

First published in Great Britain by Red Fox 2000

Printed in China

THE RANDOM HOUSE GROUP Limited Reg. No. 954009
www.randomhouse.co.uk

ISBN 0 09 940914 3

THE LITTLE
BOOK OF

Judy Hindley and
Margaret Chamberlain

Wherever I go,
I look for cats –
cats are my
favourite things.

Soppy,
floppy,
old cats,

shy cats,

bold

cats,

cosy

cats,

nosy cats –

Big,
rough
tomcats,

roly~poly
mum cats,

pretty little kitty cats,

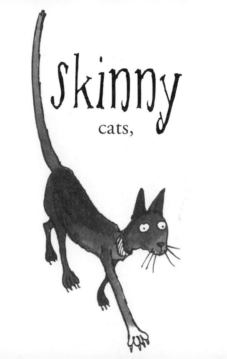

skinny

cats,

many cats,

happy

cats,

loyal cats,

dozy

cats,

royal cats,

stay-at-home-tame cats,

groovy, ravy, stray cats.

Clean cats,

slob cats,

bald cats,

bobcats,

lurking-near-the-hob cats –
any one would do!

Cats that bounce

and

pounce

and

play,

cats that sit in
the sun all day.

Tatty,

scatty,

crazy cats,

cute cats...

...lazy cats.

Howling,
yowling,
rowdy cats,

scared

cats,

proud

cats.

Lost cats,

found cats,

square cats,

round cats,

cats in collars,

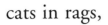

cats in rags,

cats in coats,

cats in bags,

stalking down
a butterfly,

streaking up a stair,

up a tree,   on your lap,

on a knee,   through a gap,

 on a broom,

in a box,

round a bin,

in your socks!

Keen cats,

kissing cats,

mean cats,

licking,
lapping,
drinking
cats,

prinking cats,

thinking cats.

Cats that linger,

cats that

leap,

cats that hunt,

cats asleep,

spotty,

tabby,

tiger-striped,

sugar~white,

Dippy, trippy, dozy cats,

prim cats,

posey cats,

fabulously

fat

cats,

and very
nearly flat cats,

scooting-through-
the-flap cats,

or sitting-on-
a-mat cats.

Cats that preen

PUR-R-R-R-R-R-R

and cats that purr,

cats that cuddle,

cats...

like her!

Tough cats,

rough cats,

little-ball-of-
fluff cats,

glad
cats,

bad

cats,

mad cats,

sad cats,

singing-on-the-roof cats,

and fiendishly
aloof cats.

Wherever they are at,
cats are what I truly love...

Amazing
Cat Facts

The greenest cat in the
world was born in
Denmark in 1996.
Yes, its fur is green!

The largest litter?
A four-year-old cat had
nineteen kittens in 1970.

Tom, a black and white cat, stowed away in the hold of a BA jet and flew half a million miles in two months. Among its stopovers were Australia, Jamaica and Kuwait – not bad for a cat.

Towser, who lives in
Scotland, is the best
mouser in the world. He's
caught over 28,899 mice –
an average of three a day.

Old Snowbie, the
longest cat in the world,
measures 1.03 metres
(3 ft 41/2 in) from nose
to tail, and lives
in Aberdeenshire.

CHOOSING
A CAT

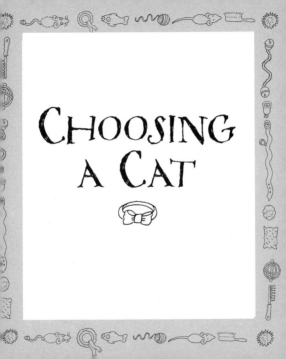

A hairy cat or a bald cat, a pedigree cat or a moggy? Cats come in all shapes and sizes –

it's up to you to choose!

A cat's for you unless...

you have a big dog
who's head of the roost...

you want to train
your cat to sit,
stay and fetch...

or you want your cat
to be snug and cuddly
ALL the time.

FEEDING
YOUR CAT

Cats love their food,
canned or dry. Feed
them at the
same time every
day, and
give them
plenty of
water too.

Milk is a welcome treat, but too much will upset your cat's tummy.

Well-fed cats stick
close to home; peckish
cats hunt far and wide.

Meat is a staple in
every cat's diet...

...so be proud when
your cat brings home
its first delicious bird
or mouse dinner.

Yum, yum!

If your cat's on
the chubby side, you
can bet it's
been getting a
titbit or two
on the sly!

GROOMING YOUR CAT

Cats bathe themselves
every day.

And cats like to nap in
the sun – sixteen hours
a day! When your
cat licks its fur clean,
just think of all the
vitamin D it will glean.

Brush daily to give your cat a clean, shiny coat and to avoid nasty matting or knotting.

Don't worry about baths
unless your cat has extra
long hair. Then take it
regularly to be properly
coiffed.

When your cat's all
clean and shiny, give it
a smart collar with your
name and number. Now
you can be sure it will
always find its
way home.

Cats and kittens love
to play. Just give
them something that
moves and they're off
and away.

A ball...

a piece of paper, a toy
mouse, or a ball of wool...

And if your cat's older,

find it a comfy place
for a good catnap…

or give it a good
stroke right under
its chin.

PUR-R-R-R

CAT
JOKES

What do cats eat
for breakfast?
Mewsli

What kind of exercise
do cats like most?
Puss-ups

When is it unlucky to see
a black cat?
When you're a mouse.

What do cats
strive for?

Pur-r-rfection

What's the name of
your kitten?
I don't know, it
won't tell me.

What do cats read
every morning?
Mewspapers